# the Cheetah Girls
## One World

# the Cheetah Girls One World

The Junior Novel
Adapted by Kirsten Larsen
Based upon the series of books by Deborah Gregory

Based on the Disney Channel Original Movie, "One World,"
Teleplay by Dan Berendsen and Nisha Ganatra & Jen Small
Story by Dan Berendsen

New York

Printed in the United States of America

First Edition
1 3 5 7 9 10 8 6 4 2

Library of Congress Control Number: 2008925671

ISBN 1-4231-1200-6

For more Disney Press fun, visit www.disneybooks.com
Visit DisneyChannel.com

# the Cheetah Girls
## One World

*The* Cheetah Girls stood at the top of a grand staircase, colored lights washing over them. As the cameras rolled, they began their descent, dancing and singing their way down the stairs. They were shooting the video for their latest hit single, "Cheetah Love," and every detail—from the smoke effects to their fabulous outfits—was nothing short of dazzling.

At the bottom of the stairs, the girls were

*mobbed by paparazzi and fans. Flashbulbs popped all around them, and gorgeous guys fell over themselves begging the Cheetahs for a chance—or even a glance. The Cheetah Girls were the hottest girl group around, and they had the world at their feet.*

*The girls wrapped up the song with a dramatic flourish. They had it. They were totally in the zone. They were . . .*

"Ooof," Chanel Simmons grunted, as she bumped into Dorinda Thomas, who then crashed into Aquanette Walker. Dorinda and Aqua both fell to the ground.

The smoke clouds of Chanel's daydream cleared to reveal that there were no colored lights, no paparazzi, and definitely no cute guys. Chanel was standing on a dirty stage in a run-down old theater, and the only people looking at her were Aqua and Dorinda—who were both glaring at her from the floor.

"Sorry," Chanel said, helping her band-mates up.

"Chanel!" Dorinda snapped. "You were supposed to turn left!"

"I did!" Chanel shot back.

"That would be your *other* left," Aqua said, demonstrating—and accidentally smacking into Dorinda.

"And *that* would be my leg," Dorinda complained. She rubbed the spot that Aqua had bumped into.

"Sorry," Aqua mumbled.

"Cheetahs?" A voice interrupted their argument.

*Oops!* The girls suddenly remembered that they were in the middle of an audition. Marty, their potential agent, was watching them with his arms crossed in front of him. And he did not look amused.

"We're still working the kinks out," Chanel quickly explained. She patted down her caramel-colored curls, trying to appear as if she had it together. "We used to be a four-some, but Galleria got into Cambridge."

"Which, you know, is great and amazing," Dorinda added.

"Especially considering her study habits," Aqua remarked dryly.

"Uh-huh." Dorinda nodded. "That's why they're making her take summer school."

Just a month before, the Cheetahs had graduated from high school, and Galleria Garibaldi had already left for college in England. Now the remaining girls were determined to prove that even though they were one Cheetah short, they still had growl power!

"But trust us," Chanel told Marty. "We totally got this down." The three Cheetahs gave him their most winning smiles.

Marty frowned. "I'm looking for a foursome," he said.

The girls' smiles sank.

"Look," the agent said, taking pity on them, "if you guys land a job, maybe we can talk about representation." He turned on the heel of his well-polished shoe and hustled out of the theater.

"Thanks," Chanel called after him.

The girls looked at one another. This wasn't good news at all.

"Now what?" asked Dorinda.

"It just seems so hopeless," Aqua sighed, as the girls started to pack up their gear.

Chanel frowned. She always believed that the Cheetahs had to think positive—*and* think big. But it seemed hopeless. In order to get an agent, they had to land a gig. But how were they supposed to get a gig without an agent? It was like some kind of riddle, Chanel thought. One that wasn't particularly funny.

As Aqua loaded her laptop into her bag, Dorinda stopped and stared. The laptop looked more like a clunky piece of machinery than an actual computer. A few parts tumbled from her bag.

"You building a robot out of your laptop?" she asked Aqua.

"Close." Aqua popped the pieces back together and gave Dorinda a sheepish look.

Dorinda's eyes narrowed suspiciously. "You are *not* messing with your computer so you can call and flirt with that tech-support guy," she challenged.

"No . . . maybe," Aqua confessed. "He has a name, you know. Kevin. Extension 347."

"What's your dad going to to say when he finds out that you're spending precious study time flirting with the geek squad?" Dorinda asked. Aqua was as smart as she was gorgeous. She'd been accepted to Columbia University in the fall, and her classes were so intense that she was already preparing for them, even though school hadn't started yet.

"Well, we can't all have a gorgeous, devoted Spanish boyfriend," Aqua teased gently, referring to Joaquin, Dorinda's long-distance beau, whom she'd met in Barcelona the summer before.

Dorinda looked down. "Actually, now no

one has a gorgeous, devoted Spanish boyfriend," she admitted.

"What?" Aqua glanced over at Chanel, who was giving her a "way to go" look. Suddenly, she got the picture: Dorinda and Joaquin had broken up.

"Oh, Do, I'm so sorry," Aqua said, calling Dorinda by her nickname. She rushed to put her arms around her friend.

But Dorinda shrugged her off. "I'm okay," she said. But she didn't sound okay at all.

Chanel and Aqua exchanged glances. They could tell when their friend was upset.

"Seriously, I'm okay," Dorinda told them.

"Yeah. You keep saying that," Chanel pointed out gently.

"What happened?" Aqua asked.

Dorinda shrugged. "Time differences, phone bills. I'm here, he's there. Things changed. It just . . . got to be too hard."

"I'm sorry, sweetie. I know how much you liked him," Chanel said softly.

But Dorinda didn't want sympathy. As a foster child, she'd been through worse things than this. She was tough, and she wasn't going to let some guy get her down.

Dorinda flipped back her long, blonde hair. "I'm cool. And hungry," she added, changing the subject. "Anyone else hungry?"

Aqua knew her friend was looking for an out, so she gave it to her. "Starving, as usual," she said. "Let's get out of here."

"You pick, Do," Chanel said. "Whatever you want."

"Anything but Spanish," Dorinda said with a half smile.

Chanel and Aqua grinned and threw their arms around her. Together the three headed out the door.

*D*owntown, in Manhattan's hip, bustling East Village, the Cheetahs found the perfect spot for chasing the blues away: a tiny Indian restaurant decked out in colorful streamers, blinking lights, and other kitschy decorations.

As she walked through the door, Dorinda passed an odd statue of a four-armed man with the head of an elephant.

Suddenly she did a double take. Did that

statue just *wink* at me? Dorinda thought.

She stopped and examined it more closely. But the statue remained as still as . . . well, as a statue.

Dorinda shook her head. All the stress must be getting to me, she thought. She hurried to catch up with her friends, who were already seated in a booth.

A beautiful, older Indian woman glided over to their table with a stack of menus. "I see you've met Ganesh," she said, smiling at Dorinda.

"The statue?" Dorinda asked.

"He's known as the remover of obstacles," the woman explained.

"That's perfect," Dorinda told her, "because we've got nothing *but* obstacles."

"Such as?" the woman asked.

"No work," Chanel told her.

"No agent," Aqua added.

"No singing career," Dorinda said with a sigh.

The woman gave them a knowing smile.

"Sometimes all you need is a little faith," she said. She placed the menus on the table, then walked away, pausing to lay a flower on the statue of Ganesh.

Aqua sighed. "This is depressing," she said, reaching for a menu. "We've been on a million auditions, and what have we booked?"

"That would be nothing," Dorinda quipped.

Aqua rubbed her temples. "I can't deal with the stress of failure when I'm already behind in my reading for Columbia," she said.

"We all start college in two months," Chanel remarked. She could hardly believe it was happening so soon.

"And once college starts, we're not going to have any time to practice," Aqua pointed out.

"Maybe it's time for things to change," Dorinda said. "I *do* have a dance-camp job lined up this summer."

Chanel looked over at Dorinda sadly. She knew Dorinda needed a job to earn money for college. Still, just hearing the word *change* made her stomach twist into a knot. It was bad enough that Galleria was already gone. Were the rest of the Cheetahs headed their own way, too?

"I don't want things to change, do you?" she asked her friends. "Are you seriously ready to give up on the Cheetah dream?"

Aqua and Dorinda looked at each other.

"I don't want it to end," Aqua admitted. Dorinda nodded in agreement.

"It's now or never," Chanel said fiercely. "So let's make it now. And from now on, I promise to be completely focused. Nothing can get in our way."

"Nothing," Aqua agreed.

"*Nada*," Chanel added for emphasis.

Just then, Chanel's cell phone rang. She flipped it open and answered it. She paused, listening. "Um, okay. Are you kidding? Of course, we're interested!"

"What? Who is it?" Dorinda whispered impatiently.

Chanel suddenly screamed. "You'd like us to audition? For a movie? Where?" she shrieked.

*A movie?* Aqua and Dorinda leaned forward, practically ready to grab the phone out of Chanel's hand.

Chanel covered the phone for a moment. "Someone wants The Cheetah Girls to star in a big Hollywood musical!" she exclaimed. She went back to her phone call and said, "Of course we'll be there!"

Chanel hung up. The Cheetahs looked at each other and screamed.

"What's the movie?" asked Aqua, breathless with excitement.

Chanel shook her head. "I can't remember. I had a little trouble focusing after the Hollywood part."

"Yeah!" all three girls shrieked.

"I haven't been this nervous in a long time," Dorinda said.

"We have to get this," Aqua said with determination.

"We will," Chanel said confidently. "I can feel it. Our luck is about to change."

They were going to nail this audition! Dorinda thought to herself. Then she hopped to her feet.

"Then what are we sitting here for?" she asked. The girls all beamed at each other. They were going to audition for a Hollywood movie!

The next day, the Cheetahs strutted into the movie audition, ready to pounce. On the stage of a darkened theater, they powered through their song as if they had been born to sing it. As they hit the final note, Chanel half expected the movie director to stand up and cheer. Who could turn them down after a performance like that?

The girls held their poses, expectant

smiles plastered on their faces.

"Just give us a moment, please," the director said gruffly. He began to mumble to someone sitting next to him. Chanel tried to peer past the spotlight shining in her eyes, but she couldn't even tell where the director was sitting in the darkened room.

"I *so* want to go to California," Dorinda whispered to her friends.

"We *are* going to California," Chanel insisted. "We were amazing."

"Shhh!" Aqua warned them. "Someone's coming."

The director stepped into the light. He was a young man dressed in casually hip clothes.

"Hi! Thank you for coming. I'm the director," he said nervously. "Well, I'm Vik. Actually, my parents call me Vikram, but I prefer Vik," he continued, taking a deep breath. "So anyway, I'm Vik. The director."

The girls glanced at each other and smiled. Did this guy ever stop talking?

He's a lot younger than I thought he'd be, Chanel thought, eyeing his tousled black hair. Younger *and* cuter!

The assistant director handed Vik a clipboard. He barely glanced at it before he continued talking. "So anyway, you were very, very good. Amazing, really," he told The Cheetah Girls.

The assistant director frowned, clearly annoyed with Vik's rambling. "We have a plane to catch," he reminded Vik.

"Right," the director remembered. "So, here's the deal," Vik said. "I would like you—all of you—to star in my movie—my first movie—if that is okay with you."

There was only one way to answer: the Cheetahs let out a roof-raising scream.

"We're going to be in a movie!" Dorinda exclaimed in a sing-song voice.

"Yes! Yes! Yes!" cried Chanel, hugging everyone in sight.

She got so caught up in the moment that she

accidentally hugged Vik before realizing what she was doing.

As she pulled away, blushing, their eyes met. Chanel felt a spark. Quickly she looked away.

"Thank you, thank you, thank you," Aqua gushed. She looked as though she wanted to hug Vik, too. "You have no idea how much this means to us."

"No, thank *you*," Vik said enthusiastically. "I'd be packing my bags for dental school if it weren't for you."

The Cheetahs glanced at one another. *What?*

"Nothing . . . it's just, my parents . . ." Vik stuttered. "Oh, never mind. So, you're cool with the schedule, right?" he asked, suddenly becoming businesslike. "Your flight leaves the day after tomorrow. Things move fast in Bollywood."

Dorinda was doing a celebration dance and singing loudly. "The Cheetahs are going to

Holly—what did he say?" she broke off, staring at Vik.

"Bollywood," Vik repeated.

Suddenly Dorinda didn't look quite so happy.

"India? Bollywood? The moviemaking capital of the world?" Vik looked from one stunned face to the next.

"*India*, India? The-other-side-of-the-world India?" Dorinda squeaked. Somewhere there had been a serious communication breakdown!

"Chanel!" Aqua cried accusingly. She and Dorinda turned to glare at her.

Chanel gave them an apologetic look. "Bollywood. Hollywood. My cell connection wasn't that good. *Ay, estúpido mobile*," she added, shaking her phone.

"I'm positive I said that we'd be shooting the movie in Mumbai," Vik said.

"In my defense, I don't actually know where Mumbai *is*," Chanel told him.

"It's the biggest city in India!" Aqua screeched.

"You'll love it," Vik assured them. "I mean, I hope you'll love it—"

Aqua turned to Vik. "Look, we're really sorry, but—"

"Why are we sorry?" Chanel cut in. "We're not sorry."

"Is there a problem?" Vik asked. "There can't be a problem. I don't have time for a problem," he added nervously.

Aqua nodded. "Yes, there's a—"

"No problem!" Chanel interrupted. "Just give us a minute." She gave Vik a brilliant smile and then pulled the other Cheetahs into a huddle. "Come on!" she whispered. "This is the chance of a lifetime."

"India is on the other side of the world!" Dorinda whispered back.

"Yeah, I thought we were going to try to make it big on *this* side of the world first. I have college prep class here this summer!" Aqua exclaimed.

"And I'm teaching dance camp," Dorinda added.

"College prep class? Dance camp?" Chanel looked at them as if they were crazy. "The Cheetahs could be international movie stars. How can we pass this up?"

Aqua looked at Chanel intently. "You're serious. You really think we should do this, huh?" she asked.

"I've never been more sure about anything," Chanel told her. "This is our Cheetah destiny."

The girls all looked at each other. Then Dorinda broke into a smile. "It *is* the movie-making capital of the world," she said.

"I guess I could get a lot of studying done on the plane," Aqua said slowly.

Dorinda nodded. "And maybe I can teach the second session at the dance camp."

"And," Chanel said, grinning, "that director is supercute!"

"I know!" Dorinda whispered. Then she started to shake her head. "Wait, uh-uh. No. I don't want to hear one thing about boys, supercute or not."

"Okay," Chanel agreed. She didn't care what the rules were, as long as they were going. "No talk about boys. Anything else?"

"Just one thing," Aqua said, a slow grin spreading across her face.

The other two knew exactly what she was going to say. "We're going to India!" they all shouted.

As the girls danced around and hugged one another, Vik's assistant director pulled him aside. "*One* girl, Vik," he hissed. "You're supposed to bring *one* girl. What's your uncle going to say when you show up with three?"

"Once my uncle meets them, he'll see that they should all be in the movie," Vik replied with a nonchalant wave of his hand.

"Uh-huh," the assistant director said uncertainly. "Do you maybe just want to talk to your uncle before you make this decision?"

"Look," said Vik, "The Cheetah Girls are

my stars. I'll just rewrite the script for three lead roles. Why do I need to talk to my uncle?"

"Uh, because he's the producer, and he's paying for the movie," he pointed out.

Vik's face fell. "Right," he said. "There's always that."

He glanced over at The Cheetah Girls, who were still talking excitedly. When Chanel caught him looking, she smiled. Vik smiled back anxiously.

*It'll all be okay*, he told himself. *I hope . . .*

*D*orinda gazed out of the window as the plane began its descent. Below, she could see a patchwork landscape of brown and green bordered by a bright blue sea.

"It's going to be nice getting out of the city for the summer," she commented.

"I know. It's so hot and crowded in New York," Chanel agreed.

In her aisle seat, Aqua looked up from her

biology book. "Hello! Does anybody besides me watch the Weather Channel?" She shook her head. The weather in Mumbai was going to be even hotter!

A short time later, the girls realized exactly what Aqua meant. Squished together in the back of a yellow-and-black cab decorated with bright flowers and multicolored wheels, they swerved through the jam-packed streets of Mumbai. Horns blared, tires screeched, and drivers shouted. Mumbai was way beyond crowded—it was total chaos!

Suddenly Dorinda grabbed her friends' hands. They were on a collision course with an elephant!

"Watch out!" she screamed. The Cheetahs all shut their eyes and braced for the crash.

But thankfully it never came. Dorinda opened her eyes. At the last second, the cab driver had swerved around the elephant. As they passed it, Dorinda stared.

Was the elephant looking at her? She

shook her head. Maybe I have jet lag, she thought.

Suddenly, her cell phone rang. She flipped it open and saw Joaquin's name pop up on the screen.

She quickly hit IGNORE. The last thing she needed was a boy ruining her first look at a whole new continent.

Aqua and Chanel finally opened their eyes. They looked at Dorinda and smiled.

"Okay, so it's hot and crowded," Chanel admitted.

"But we're in India!" Dorinda exclaimed.

"And it's Cheetah-licious!" Aqua cried.

Moments later, the driver pulled up in front of an ornate old hotel. The Cheetahs climbed out of the cab to check out their new home for the summer. Dorinda looked around in amazement.

"Loving Mumbai," she decided. "Beautiful hotel."

"Room service," Aqua noted with a nod, as

she spotted tables of food sitting under a nearby tent.

"And jewelry for sale right near the front door," said Chanel, eyeing a nearby open-air market.

The girls smiled and headed inside the hotel. Chanel, having brought the most luggage, lagged behind for a moment.

They started to pick up their bags, but a bellhop beat them to it. They followed him in, talking excitedly. But the girls fell silent when the saw the hotel lobby—it looked like a palace!

I knew coming here was the right thing, Chanel thought, smiling with satisfaction.

*L*ater that afternoon, the girls left the hotel to check out the jewelry at the market. They couldn't believe how cheap everything was. Mumbai was a shopper's paradise! Chanel bought a statue of the Taj Mahal for her mother, Juanita. "My mom will love this," she told Dorinda.

Dorinda smiled and wandered into another

tent. As she walked, she noticed a large tree with hundreds of red strings tied to its branches. A Swami, who according to Hindu culture is a master of yoga, sat underneath the tree, meditating. He was wearing a bright orange robe, and he had his eyes closed.

As Dorinda passed him, the man's eyes suddenly snapped open. "You!" he shouted. "Take this string and tie it in the tree." He held out a red string.

Mumbai is like New York after all, Dorinda thought. Crazies and everything. "Don't get me wrong," she told the man politely, deciding that the best strategy was to pretend he was sane. "It's colorful and all, but I think there are enough strings."

"It's for a wish," the Swami persisted. "You make a wish, tie the string, and when it comes true, you return and untie the string. And say thank you."

"To the tree?" Dorinda asked incredulously. Yep, crazy, she thought.

"Who else?" the Swami asked, looking at Chanel and Aqua.

"Come on, Cheetahs," Chanel said, over-hearing them. "We can use the good luck. Everyone make a wish."

Each of the Cheetahs took a string and tied it to the tree, silently making their wishes. The Swami smiled with satisfaction. Then he closed his eyes and went back to meditating.

*T*he next morning, Dorinda was up early. Still in her pajamas, she sat in a window seat, leafing through her Cheetah Girls scrap-book. Looking up for moment, Dorinda caught a glimpse of a nearby Ganesh statue. Oddly, it seemed as if his eyes were following her. Not again, she thought, and turned to look out the window. She smiled at the sight of the turquoise water in the distance. This was the life!

"I can't believe a girl from New York is

standing here looking out at the Indian Ocean," she murmured.

"Arabian Sea," Aqua said, correcting her, as she walked into the room.

Dorinda rolled her eyes. Aqua, aka Einstein-ette, always had all the answers!

"Pardon me for cracking a guidebook," Aqua replied innocently. She held up her cell phone. "Hey, do you think I can call Kevin 347 now? Because it's night back home. Or should I wait for tonight, which I guess would be yesterday?"

Dorinda wasn't even going to try to figure that one out. "Honestly, why are you wasting your time?" she asked. "Phone relationships are doomed."

"You used to think it was romantic," Aqua reminded her.

"Learn from my mistakes," said Dorinda.

Just then Chanel came out of her room, looking at her PDA. "Ready for your close-ups, *amigas* Cheetahs?" she asked excitedly.

"Vik just sent over the rehearsal schedule, and if we don't hurry, we're going to be late for rehearsal."

"We're going to be stars!" Dorinda exclaimed with a grin.

"Hey," Aqua said, turning to Chanel. "Thank you."

"For what?" asked Chanel.

"For believing in the Cheetahs," said Aqua.

Dorinda nodded. "If it wasn't for you, we wouldn't be here. You were fierce."

"You know there's nothing that I wouldn't do to keep my girls together," Chanel replied. She looked at the other Cheetahs and smiled.

Dorinda threw her fists in the air. "Bollywood, here we come!"

*5*

*T*he Cheetahs' cab pulled up in front of
the studio gates. Chanel introduced herself
and the other Cheetahs to the guard. "The
Cheetah Girls," she said with a smile.

The guard started checking the list, while
the girls stood there in awe.

"I can't believe this is really happening,"
Aqua said breathlessly.

"It's amazing," Dorinda commented.

"*Better* than amazing," said Chanel.

The guard waved them in, and their driver slowly drove into the studio lot. The Cheetahs stared in wonder. Through the windows they could see trucks full of equipment, crew members busy at work, and groups of costumed dancers rehearsing. Everything looked exactly as they'd imagined a movie studio would.

The car dropped them off at the entrance to the back lot. The trio climbed out and found themselves standing in front of a painting of an elaborate Indian palace.

"The Taj Mahal," Aqua said reverently. "Built in 1643. One of the seven wonders of the world."

"*And* the most romantic place in all of India," a male voice added.

Two crew members suddenly picked up the painted backdrop and carried it away, revealing Vik standing behind it.

"They say if you kiss someone there at sunset, you'll know in your heart if your love is true," Vik told them.

"Count me out," Dorinda said sourly. Chanel elbowed her.

But Vik barely seemed to notice Dorinda's remark. His eyes were on Chanel. "Glad you made it," he said, smiling.

"Me, too," Chanel replied, blushing.

"Shall we?" Vik said, turning to the others. He began to lead them on a tour of the busy studio.

"So I really wanted to do a more traditional remake of the classic hit *Namaste Bombay*," Vik explained as they walked. "But my uncle, the producer—well, it was his idea to make it more marketable. Cast Americans, make it more modern, more contemporary.'"

"What's the script about, anyway?" Dorinda asked.

"Ah, well, there are still a couple of adjustments we need to make, but basically it's a love story," Vik said.

"I love romance," Chanel said dreamily. Her gaze met Vik's. This time *he* was the one who blushed. Dorinda rolled her eyes.

"I can't wait to tell Kevin about our movie," Aqua chimed in.

"Hello?" Dorinda huffed. "Does anyone remember our deal? No boy talk."

But no one was paying attention to her. "It's classic Bollywood cinema," Vik explained, "which is all singing, dancing, romance, and intrigue."

He stopped beside a wall of framed movie posters. "That's Rahim," he said, pointing to a really cute guy in one of the posters. "He's your co-star."

"He's our *co-star*?" Aqua cried. She whipped a copy of *Bollywood Star* out of her bag and showed her friends the picture of Rahim on its cover. "He's one of the biggest stars. Bollywood royalty!"

Vik nodded. "And my uncle gave him his first movie. Here he comes now," he said, pointing.

The girls turned to see Rahim riding toward

them on a flashy motorcycle. As he pulled into the studio lot, he was mobbed by a group of screaming fans who were waiting for him, all waving their autograph books and pens. Rahim pulled to a stop and casually took a pen from a fan's hand, as if this happened every day. Which, the Cheetahs realized, it probably did.

"Who should I make this out to?" he asked one of the excited girls in the crowd.

"My mom. No, me! No, my mom!" she spluttered. "She loved your parents in *Namaste Bombay*. It's so romantic that they fell in love while filming."

"Yes, it is very romantic. Thank you," Rahim said politely. "Next, please?"

His eyes fell on another girl, who was so stunned that she could barely move. She just stood there with her mouth hanging open, staring at Rahim. At last, she managed to hold out her autograph book.

Dorinda leaned over to Chanel. "That is so embarrassing!" she whispered.

"I know," Chanel agreed. "She needs to act like the grown woman she is!"

When he had finished signing autographs, Rahim walked over to The Cheetah Girls.

"Rahim," Vik greeted him, "meet your co-leads: Chanel, Dorinda, and Aqua."

The girls all froze. Rahim was gorgeous! He had silky black hair, shining brown eyes, and a dazzlingly white smile. For a moment, all they could do was stare.

"Nice to meet you," said Rahim casually. "I hear you're great. I'm looking forward to working with you." He held out his hand.

But none of the girls took it. They were still too busy staring at him. Finally, Rahim pulled his hand back.

Vik cleared his throat. "Well, if you'll excuse me, I have to get busy writing—uh, well, re-writing." He bustled off just as his assistant director walked up.

"Come on, ladies," the assistant director said. "They're ready for you."

The girls shook themselves out of their Rahim-inspired daze and followed the assistant director inside, with Rahim walking behind them. The Cheetah Girls were psyched! It was time to show Bollywood what they were all about!

*6*

*A*s they approached the set, the assistant director explained that the big dance scene would be shot in front of a spectacular palace. However, when they arrived at the dance rehearsal space, Chanel couldn't help feeling disappointed. The cheap palace backdrop didn't look very regal, despite the efforts of the crew that was working to spruce it up.

From somewhere in the distance, Chanel

could hear a loud voice complaining, "I don't understand. These Americans are supposed to be on time!"

At that moment, a beautiful woman with long black hair strode onto the set. She spotted the Cheetahs and glared in their direction. "Ladies," she snapped, "I can't spend half my day chasing after my act—"

She broke off suddenly when she spotted Rahim. "Oh, Rahim. Hi," she said, her tone changing completely. "I didn't know . . ."

Suddenly, there was a loud crash. The woman tripped over a folding chair. As she tried to regain her balance, she somehow got stuck in it.

"That's Gita. She's our choreographer," Rahim told the Cheetahs, without taking his eyes off her.

"*She's* the choreographer?" Dorinda asked worriedly. Based on the tango that Gita was currently doing with the chair, her moves didn't inspire a lot of confidence!

Rahim hurried over to help Gita—and he tripped, too. As they both flailed around, Rahim tried to stifle a giggle but ended up snorting instead. He looked at Gita, mortified.

Finally, the assistant director rescued them. "Rahim," he hissed, grabbing the actor's arm, "you've got a costume fitting. Excuse us, ladies." He nodded at the Cheetahs and hustled Rahim out of the room.

The Cheetahs exchanged looks. "Did he just snort?" asked Dorinda.

"Twice," Chanel said.

Aqua chuckled. "Okay, kind of over him."

*W*hen Gita finally managed to compose herself, she led the Cheetahs to the dance rehearsal area. Dozens of men and women were there, waiting for the rehearsal to start, and they looked very impatient.

"Okay, listen up," Gita called to the group of dancers. "I've managed to track down our *stars*."

The Cheetahs couldn't help noticing how

she sneered while pronouncing the word.

Gita gestured to the three girls. "This is . . ."

"—Aqua—"

"—Dorinda—"

"—Chanel—"

The Cheetahs grinned at the group, who returned their smiles with icy stares.

"And these are your dancers," Gita said quickly. "Vik says you are amazing dancers, so you shouldn't have any trouble picking it up."

The Cheetahs took their places, ready to bust out all their best moves.

Unfortunately, the second Gita started dancing it became obvious that her style was totally different from theirs. As she whipped through a series of classical Indian dance moves, the Cheetahs struggled to keep up.

"So it's just step, turn, head back, turn, turn, turn," Gita explained. "Bollywood 101."

"What if you've never taken *Bollywood 1*?" Chanel whispered to Dorinda.

"Is it all going to be like this?" Aqua

muttered from Dorinda's other side.

"Okay, and—" Gita shouted, "five, six, seven, eight!"

The music started. The Cheetahs did their best, but they were only steps into the dance when it completely fell apart. Aqua turned left when everyone else turned right. She crashed into Chanel, who backed up and accidentally tripped Dorinda. They landed in a pile on the floor.

"Hold it, hold it, hold it," Gita said impatiently.

"Sorry. Sorry," Aqua mumbled. "It's just that we've never done this before."

"Yeah, I can see that," Gita commented.

Dorinda's eyes narrowed. She hopped to her feet and brushed herself off. "Are you saying you don't think we can dance?"

"It's okay," Gita replied coolly. "My job is to make sure you look like you can dance, even if you can't."

Chanel and Aqua cast a worried look at

Dorinda, who looked as if she were about to explode. Gita turned back to the other dancers. "All right, people. We're going to have to break it down even more. A *lot* more."

"Okay, that is it!" Dorinda snarled. She was going to kick some Bollywood butt!

But her friends held her back. "*Calmate, Chica!* She's the choreographer. It's her vision," Chanel said.

"We'll figure it out," Aqua added. "It's new."

"I know. You're right," said Dorinda in exasperation. "But nobody tells me I can't dance." She marched over to Gita.

"Let's see your moves," Dorinda challenged.

Gita smirked and took the floor, with her whole crew of dancers behind her. The Cheetahs watched as they began to dance. Their moves were strong yet graceful, and the choreography was precise.

Finally, they came to a stop. Gita gave Dorinda a look that said, "Top that!"

The Cheetahs approached some of Gita's dancers and pulled out all of their fiercest moves. It might not have been Gita's style of dancing, but there was no doubt about the fact that the Cheetahs could *move*.

But then something amazing happened. Suddenly, everyone started dancing together, their moves somehow synchronizing perfectly. The East-West combination style was flawless. By the time the music ended, everyone was out of breath.

Gita gave the Cheetahs a sheepish grin. "Okay, so I was wrong," she admitted. "You *can* dance."

"You're not so bad yourself," said Dorinda.

Gita laughed and gave her a hug.

"Do, your moves are gonna turn Bollywood out!" Chanel exclaimed.

Just then, Vik's Uncle Kamal, the film's producer, came running over. "What is going on here?" he demanded. He glared at the Cheetahs. "Who are you?"

"We're the stars of the movie," Dorinda told him.

"Stars?" he growled.

At that moment, Vik and the assistant director rounded the corner. Vik was carrying a revised script. When he spotted his uncle talking to the Cheetahs, he dropped the script and ducked for cover behind his assistant.

"Vikram Kumar Bhatia!" Kamal bellowed. "*Ek . . . bas en* American actress."

"Yes, Uncleji?" Vik peeped.

"One star!" Kamal held up one finger and waved it at Vik. "Your script has one star! Your *budget* has one star."

"I made a couple of changes," Vik said meekly.

"Well, the budget hasn't changed!" Kamal boomed.

"What?" Dorinda exclaimed.

"But there are three of us!" Aqua cried. The Cheetahs looked at each other in confusion. They'd flown all the way to India for a movie all three of them weren't supposed to be in?

"Uncle, listen," Vik pleaded. "They are fantastic. If you would just take a moment to watch them perform, I'm sure you'll see."

Kamal folded his arms. "Good idea," he said finally.

"But, I—what?" Vik did a double take. "Excuse me?"

"Each Cheetah performs," Kamal decided. "Then I'll pick the best one."

"You mean, like, an audition? As in, against one another?" Aqua asked.

"That's right," said Kamal. "Then I pick one star, and the others go home. I'll give you a couple days to prepare."

Vik looked dismayed. "But I'm the director," he argued. "I . . . I . . . I spent days rewriting the script," he stuttered.

"Do you want to make a movie, or shall I call your parents and tell them you would rather be a dentist?" Kamal asked his nephew threateningly.

Vik sighed. "I'll start rewriting. Again," he added.

"Another good idea," Kamal said. He nodded to the Cheetahs. "Ladies," he said, before striding out of the room.

The Cheetahs all stared at one another. None of them could believe what had just happened.

Aqua turned to Vik. "What was he talking about?" she demanded. "We're a group. You cast the Cheetahs. Plural."

"We're together," Dorinda added. "You can't take one and not the others."

"I know that this must be a little bit shocking. . . ." Vik began.

"That's an understatement," Chanel snapped.

"No deal," Dorinda told Vik. "Come on, Cheetahs. We're out of here." She turned and the other two Cheetahs followed her out of the room.

Vik looked at them as they walked away. He felt powerless. "They didn't tell me about all this rewriting in film school," he muttered.

Moments later, the girls burst through the studio doors and hurried toward their cab.

"What were we thinking?" Dorinda exploded.

"I gave up a college prep class," Aqua groaned.

"And I could have been teaching at dance camp," Dorinda said with dismay. It seemed as if they had sacrificed so much—and it was all for nothing.

Aqua turned to Chanel. "Maybe the Cheetahs are over," she said sadly. She hurried off to their waiting car, with Dorinda close on her heels.

Chanel watched them go. She couldn't believe what a mess everything had turned out to be. And it was all her fault.

Maybe Aqua's right, she thought. Maybe it's time for The Cheetah Girls to go their separate ways.

The next day, the Cheetahs strolled through a waterfront promenade's market. Dorinda browsed through a rack of clothes, Aqua dug through a pile of silk scarves, and Chanel tried on sparkly earrings. The tension in the air was thick. The girls had barely spoken since they'd left the studio the day before. And for once, even shopping wasn't making them feel better.

At last, Chanel decided to break the ice. "So,

what do you think?" she asked the other Cheetahs.

Aqua glanced over at her. "Cute bangles," she said.

"No, about the whole auditioning thing," said Chanel.

Aqua sighed. "I don't know." She picked up a scarf and handed it to Dorinda. "What do you think?" she asked.

"I think it stinks," Dorinda replied.

"What? This color is perfect on you!" Aqua exclaimed.

"No, the auditioning thing," Dorinda said.

"Oh. Yeah, it does," Aqua agreed. "They don't think we're actually going to compete with each other, *do* they?"

"I'm really sorry I got us into this mess," Chanel said. She paused and then turned to Dorinda. "Do, I think you should take the role. After all, you actually turned down a job to do this, and you really need the money."

"No, Aqua, *you* should do it," Dorinda

argued. "This is your chance to show what a great actress you are."

Aqua shook her head. "No, Vik clearly wants Chanel."

"What?" Chanel exclaimed.

"Come on," Aqua said, rolling her eyes. "Vik doesn't even look at us when you're around."

Really? Chanel thought, feeling a little flutter in her stomach. But she tried to ignore it. "That's not true," she told her friends. "And even if it were true, I would never use that to get an unfair advantage over my best friends. Look, we could all do this, and it's the chance of a lifetime. Can we really pass it up?"

Aqua and Dorinda looked at each other. They were both thinking the same thing.

"I think we should do it!" Aqua declared.

"Yeah, fair and square—Cheetah style!" Dorinda exclaimed.

The girls laughed and linked arms. Just then, Aqua's cell phone rang.

Aqua checked the screen. "That's weird. No caller ID. Hello?" she said.

"Aqua?" asked a familiar voice. "This is Kevin, from Totally Tech Support. Kevin 347."

Aqua covered the phone with her hand. "It's Kevin 347!" she whispered to her friends. "He's never called *me* before!"

"Oh, my gosh! What are you doing? *Talk* to him!" Chanel commanded.

Aqua put the phone back to her ear. "I hope it's okay that I'm calling," Kevin was saying. "I was just following up on your computer problem. Were you able to fix it?"

"You were right," Aqua told him, walking away from her friends. "I just needed to defrag the disk, replace the corrupted registry file, and reload the eight-oh-two-eleven-B driver, and then it was fine."

Kevin laughed. "Okay, now I'm officially impressed," he said. "I knew you really didn't need my help."

Aqua looked out at the sun setting over

the ocean. Even though they were speaking computer jargon, she couldn't help thinking it was one of the most romantic phone conversations she'd ever had. "Is that the only reason you called?" she asked.

"Not entirely," he admitted. "Are you busy?"

"I'm not doing anything," said Aqua.

"Neither am I," he replied. "I mean, other than looking at the most beautiful sunset I've ever seen."

"It *is* beautiful," Aqua agreed, admiring a boat out on the water. Its white sail shimmered in the sunset. Suddenly Aqua scrunched up her nose as she realized something. "Wait a minute. You're watching the sunset, too?"

"That means—" Kevin began.

"We're in the same time zone!" Aqua finished for him. "Wow! There's this beautiful blue-and-red boat."

"With a white sail?" Kevin asked excitedly. "Wait a minute. Describe exactly where you are."

Aqua looked around. "I'm on a gorgeous path—"

"Along the Arabian Sea—" said Kevin.

Aqua's heart began to pound. Was it possible that Kevin 347 was actually *here*? She started walking through the crowd. "There are people out, holding hands," she told him. She looked around for a landmark. "Ooh, there's an ice-cream stand called . . ."

"Naturals?" asked Kevin.

"That's right!" Aqua took a few steps back and bumped smack into someone.

Turning around, she found herself face to face with a supercute guy, who was also talking on his cell phone.

"You didn't tell me you were coming to India," the guy said with a smile. Aqua heard it in stereo, because the same words were coming through her phone!

"You didn't tell me you *lived* in India," she replied, flipping her phone shut.

The supercute guy closed his phone too. "Aqua?" he said.

"Kevin 347?" Aqua asked in disbelief.

"Amar, actually," he told her. "I'm only Kevin at work."

Aqua couldn't stop staring. She'd never expected her call-center crush to be so *adorable*!

Just then, she remembered her friends. She glanced over at Chanel and Dorinda. They'd been watching the whole scene. "*This is HIM!*" Aqua mouthed.

Chanel grinned. She threw her arm around Dorinda and began to steer her away. "Let's give our girl a little privacy," she said.

Dorinda scowled. "I've seen how these long-distance things end," she told Chanel. "Don't you think we should warn her?"

"I think it's romantic," Chanel said dreamily. "I *knew* India was a place where anything could happen."

Dorinda folded her arms and huffed. She looked out at the busy street, where another elephant was lumbering along. As it passed them, it winked with one large brown eye. Dorinda stared.

"Have you noticed that all the elephants are looking at me?" she asked Chanel.

Chanel laughed. "Are you for real? They're elephants!"

"I'm not kidding!" Dorinda exclaimed. "They look like they want to tell me something."

Chanel put her arm around her friend. "Maybe they're trying to tell you that it's okay for your friends to have a little fun and flirt, because it doesn't mean they're going to abandon you."

"Good. Because this is our last summer together, and I'm afraid everything will change when we go off to college," Dorinda confessed.

"Don't be silly, Do," Chanel said. "We're always going to be here for each other."

"Really?" Dorinda asked. "I guess I was worried that things will change so much that

I'll lose you guys, and you're . . ."

The sound of Chanel's ringing cell phone cut her off. Chanel scooped it out of her bag. "It's Vik!" she said excitedly after flipping it open.

"Figures," Dorinda grumbled.

"I'll tell him about the audition," Chanel said.

As she stepped away to talk to Vik, Dorinda sighed. Chanel had just said they'd always be there for each other. So why did Dorinda suddenly feel so alone?

As Dorinda made her way back to the hotel, she passed the wishing tree, with the Swami still sitting beneath it. She stopped and looked at the red string she had tied to it. It gently fluttered in the breeze.

"Having doubts?" asked a nearby voice.

Dorinda jumped and spun around. The Swami was watching her. "What? Me? No," she said.

The Cheetah Girls—Dorinda, Aquanette, and Chanel—are headed to India to star in a Bollywoood musical!

Dorinda is psyched to strut her stuff—*Bollywood*-style. "We're going to be stars!" she declared.

Chanel is ready to pounce on the chance to appear on the silver screen. "Ready for your close-ups, *amigas* Cheetahs?" she asked.

"I can't believe this is really happening," Aqua said. She can't wait to show the world what true Cheetah spots are all about!

The movie's producer tells the Cheetahs that he only needs one of them to star in his film. But they won't perform unless they're a group. Or *will* they?

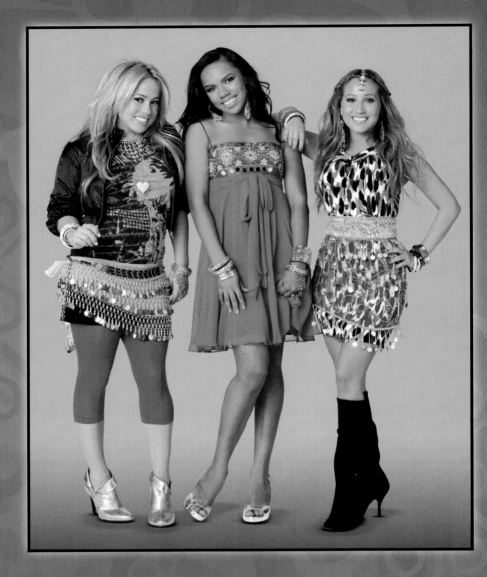

The girls decide to audition for the movie—separately.
They know that their strong Cheetah bond will never be broken.
"Fair and square—Cheetah-style," said Dorinda.

Dorinda has got the moves that will set Bollywood spinning.

Chanel has got the growl power to take her to the top.

Aqua's got the acting skills that will make Bollywood stand up and take notice.

In the end, the producer decided that
all three girls could be in the movie.

The Cheetah Girls are unstoppable!

The Swami's eyebrows lifted.

"Maybe," Dorinda confessed.

"Sometimes what we wish for isn't really what we need," the Swami said. "Don't miss where you are now because you're anxious for the future. Understand?"

"But what if I'm afraid of where I'm going?" Dorinda asked.

"Here, look at this tree," the Swami said. "The branches grow out to the sky, but the trunk remains the same. Life brings changes, but the things that are really important always stay with you."

"Not a big fan of change," Dorinda said.

"Change comes whether you want it to or not," the Swami replied. He studied Dorinda for a moment. "I can see you've been through a lot in life," he said. "So, you know that when things seem bad, they don't always stay that way. Correct?"

She shrugged. That was true. But it didn't make her feel much better just then.

The Swami reached into his bag and pulled out a tiny statue of a four-armed man with an elephant's head. He held it out to Dorinda.

Dorinda took it. "Ganesh?" she said doubtfully. "He was supposed to remove obstacles, but now we have even more. Do you have anything else that can help me?"

"Ah, yes. I have just the thing," said the Swami. He picked up a large banana leaf and raised it over Dorinda's head. "Close your eyes," he told her.

Dorinda closed her eyes. There was a whoosh of air, and the banana leaf gently batted her head. Her eyes flew open. "What was that for?"

He smiled. "Clarity," he said, and swatted her again.

*8*

The next day, Amar and Aqua strolled through the park, where dozens of food vendors could be found. As they walked past stands selling grilled meat, sticky sweets, and piles of tropical fruit, Aqua's mouth watered. She wanted to try everything!

Amar bought a paper cone full of fried dough covered with chili pepper. Aqua eagerly popped some in her mouth. Her eyes widened.

"Too spicy?" Amar asked, watching her face.

"Are you kidding?" Aqua said, reaching for another handful. "This is like breakfast in Texas. What's it called again?"

"*Chaat*," Amar told her. "*Papri chaat*, actually."

"It's like Indian nachos," Aqua said. "Crunchy, with a little bit of kick." She reached into her purse and pulled out a bottle of hot sauce and added a few drops.

Amar raised his eyebrows. "I love a girl that can handle her chilies," said Amar. "I bet you won't find this in New York."

"Maybe you can bring me some," Aqua hinted.

She noticed a group of children following them, so she stopped and bought them a bag of candy. Amar smiled at her kindness.

"You know," Aqua went on, "Columbia has one of the best physics departments in the world. . . ."

But Amar was already shaking his head. "My

father would never agree to that," he said. "It's all planned. I start at the Indian School of Business in the fall. I didn't really even have a choice."

Aqua frowned and took another handful of *chaat*. "Can't you tell him you want to keep your options open?"

"The only time I talk to my father is when I listen to him telling me what to do," Amar replied. "And he tells me I'm going into the family business. So I'm going into the family business."

"But you could be anything," Aqua argued. "You're the first guy I ever met who can explain the difference between a photon and a quark."

Amar smiled at her. "And you're the first girl I met who cares," he said.

Wow, Aqua thought, with this guy, even *physics* seems romantic. Could he be any more amazing?

"Sometimes I get frustrated that I don't have

more options," Amar told her. "But I think I'd be terrified if I had as many as you do."

"The one thing my dad has always taught me is to go after my dreams," Aqua said.

"So, what's one of your dreams?" Amar asked.

"Honestly?" Aqua said. "To star in Vik's movie."

"So, go for it!" he told her. "Don't let anyone stop you."

"Yes, but . . ." Aqua sighed.

"But what?" asked Amar.

"Well, it's a little more complicated," said Aqua. "There's only one role, and three Cheetahs want it." She stopped walking and looked at Amar. Something else had just occurred to her: if she got the role, she would get to stay here for the summer, with Amar.

Now Aqua wanted the job more than ever.

*M*eanwhile, at the studio, Dorinda was watching a dance rehearsal. Rahim was supposed to be front and center, but he was so clumsy around Gita that he kept bumping into other dancers. Gita wasn't much better. His presence had turned her from a confident choreographer into a klutz with two left feet.

It was obvious to Dorinda that the two were crazy about each other. She looked at them with amusement.

Finally, to everyone's relief, Gita called a break.

"You have got to be kidding me," Dorinda told Rahim, as she headed over to get some water.

"What?" asked Rahim, looking confused.

"You can't even rehearse!" she exclaimed. "Every time you're around her, you act like a dork."

"I do not act like a dork," said Rahim defensively.

Dorinda raised her eyebrows and nodded.

"Really? A dork?" Rahim asked, looking alarmed.

"Well, a little," Dorinda admitted. She hesitated, but then decided that Rahim needed to know the truth. "That's not true," she told him. "A lot. You're really a big dork around her."

Rahim sighed. "I know! It's just that I get so, so . . . *nervous* around her."

"Why?" asked Dorinda. "You're the big movie star."

"Because I've never felt this way before," Rahim told her.

Dorinda rolled her eyes. "That's the oldest line in the book. And I've heard it before," she said, thinking of Joaquin.

"I mean it," Rahim insisted. "I've never even kissed a girl. Ever."

Dorinda waited for him to laugh. But he was watching her nervously, waiting for her reaction.

"Oh, wow," she replied. "You're actually telling the truth."

Rahim gave her a sheepish smile.

"But I've seen you kiss . . . in your movies," Dorinda pointed out.

"Yes. On camera. But never for real. Not off camera." He fiddled with the hem of his shirt, embarrassed.

Dorinda could hardly believe what she was hearing: here was a total hottie holding out for true love! "Wow. That's actually kind of . . . romantic."

"It is?" Rahim suddenly looked hopeful. "Dorinda, would you help me?" he asked.

"What?" said Dorinda, startled. A movie star was asking *her* for help?

"Help me to not act like such a dork around Gita," he explained.

"You really like her, don't you?" Dorinda said. Rahim nodded.

The poor guy—he really does want help. . . . And I am definitely NOT the one to give it to him, Dorinda thought, coming back to her senses.

"No way!" she told Rahim. "Don't you know

that crushes lead to boyfriends, and boyfriends just break your heart?" She wasn't talking about Rahim anymore, but she couldn't stop the words from coming out of her mouth. "Sorry, bud. You're on your own."

"If you help me with Gita, I promise to help you with the audition," Rahim said.

Dorinda hesitated. "I don't know," she said.

"I've seen you dance," Rahim told her. "I can help you show the world what you can do."

Dorinda looked at Rahim. She could tell he was serious.

Maybe it's time for me to start getting serious, too, she thought.

*O*n the other side of the studio lot, Chanel was looking at Vik's new script. "You rewrote it *again*?" she asked.

"It was either rewrite the movie or—*vrrrrrrrrrrr.*" Vik made a sound like a dentist's drill. "As my uncle likes to say."

"I guess if that's what it takes to get your

movie made," Chanel said doubtfully. It seemed to her that Vik was afraid to stand up for himself.

"I know what you're thinking," Vik said, "but this is my one shot. And, yes, if I have to make some compromises, at least I get a shot at my dream. What if this was your only shot to be a star?"

Chanel glanced away. Deep down, she knew it just might be.

"Don't you think you'd give it everything you've got?" Vik went on. "I mean, how could you spend the rest of your life wondering if you could've really made it?"

Chanel inhaled sharply. She hadn't thought of that. Maybe Vik was right. Maybe she owed it to herself to go after her dream.

"Well, I have to get back to writing," Vik said. "See you later."

Chanel smiled at him. As he walked away, she thoughtfully twisted a curl around her finger. She definitely had a lot to think about.

9

"So, are you guys okay with auditioning against each other?" Gita asked Dorinda later that night.

They were strolling through the clothing vendors near The Cheetah Girls' hotel. Dorinda stopped to browse through a rack of shirts. "Yeah," she told Gita. "Look, we're best friends. We trust each other completely. No one would ever do anything to betray that just to get a part in a movie."

Gita raised one eyebrow. "Wow, that's refreshing," she commented. "Obviously, you've never worked in Bollywood."

Dorinda spotted a sparkly sequined top. "Try this on!" she told Gita, holding it out.

Gita wrinkled her nose. "I could never pull that off," she told Dorinda. "Just something plain for me." She moved over to a rack of plain-looking *kurtas*, the long shirts Indian men and woman wore.

Dorinda shrugged and put the top back. But when she turned back to her friend, Gita had disappeared.

"Gita?" she said.

"*Shhhhh!* He's here!" a voice whispered from somewhere near the ground.

Dorinda looked down. Gita was lying on her back, cowering beneath a bedding display!

*He?* Dorinda thought. He, who? Just then, she spotted a cardboard cutout of Rahim a few feet away.

Dorinda marched over, grabbed the cutout,

and stuck it under the bedding display. "Is *this* what you're worried about?" she asked Gita.

"*Aaaah!*" Gita screamed. But a second later she realized her mistake. She slowly crawled out from under the bedding and dusted herself off.

"You were saying?" she asked, trying to sound casual.

Dorinda rolled her eyes. "You can cut it out. I know you like him."

"Yeah, well, who doesn't?" Gita said defiantly. "But he would never want to go out with me. I'm not a movie star."

"Do you wish you were? You know, a star?" Dorinda asked.

Gita shrugged. "I don't know. I don't think I could ever be a star. I just love performing—acting, singing, and dancing. I've always loved to dance."

"Well, just for the record, when you dance, it's clear that you are a star," Dorinda told her. "You don't need a guy to tell you that."

Gita laughed and linked her arm through Dorinda's.

*T*he next day, Vik invited the Cheetahs to go for a boat ride on the lake in a local park. But since Aqua had plans with Amar, Chanel and Dorinda went to meet him without her.

As they approached the dock, Dorinda noticed that Vik had dressed up. Instead of his usual outfit of T-shirt and jeans, he was wearing a button-down shirt and perfectly tailored pants.

He looks like he's dressed for a date, Dorinda thought. "Are you sure he invited me?" she asked Chanel.

"Of course. It's not like this is a date or something," Chanel told her. She looked down at her own outfit and added, "Do you think I look all right? I could go home and change."

Dorinda rolled her eyes.

"I'm so glad you could make it," Vik said as they walked up to him.

"Wouldn't miss it," Dorinda told him.

"And listen," Vik said, "I'm really sorry about the whole mess with my uncle."

"I understand," Chanel said sweetly.

"You do? Thanks." An expression of relief washed over Vik's face. Vik held out his hand and helped Chanel into a small paddle boat shaped like a swan. Then he climbed in and sat down next to her.

"Yeah," said Chanel. "I know you're going to figure out how to make the movie you want to make." She and Vic exchanged glances.

Dorinda cleared her throat. Suddenly Vik and Chanel realized that she was still standing on the dock. There was room only for two in the cozy little boat.

"Thanks. I'm okay. I'll just ride alone in this one," Dorinda said pointedly, climbing into the boat behind theirs.

As Chanel and Vik paddled off together, Dorinda struggled to keep up with them. But eventually she gave up.

What am I even doing here? she thought. Paddling around by herself wasn't all that much fun.

She took her boat back to the dock. As she climbed out, she looked back at Chanel, who had her head thrown back and was laughing at something Vik was saying. The two seemed to be having a perfectly good time without her.

As Dorinda was leaving the park, her cell phone rang. She glanced at the caller ID. When she saw that it was Joaquin, she put the phone away without answering.

She thought about Chanel and Vik, Aqua and Amar, even Rahim and Gita. It seemed as if the whole world had paired up.

Everyone is in love, Dorinda thought with a sigh. Everyone but me.

*T*hat night, Dorinda was alone in the hotel room reading a magazine when Chanel and Aqua returned.

"Hey, Cheetahs," Dorinda greeted them.

Neither replied. They were both staring dreamily into space. Aqua sat down next to Dorinda. It seemed as if Aqua hadn't even realized anyone else was in the room.

"Aqua?" said Dorinda.

"Oh, hey, Do," Aqua said absently. "I didn't hear you come in."

"Did you have a good time?" Chanel asked.

"Oh, yeah," Dorinda said sarcastically. "Just call me the fifth wheel."

"That's great," said Aqua, not listening.

"Cool," Chanel added. Clearly she hadn't heard a thing Dorinda had said, either.

Chanel and Aqua both floated out of the room on their respective clouds, leaving Dorinda alone to stew.

10

The next day, Vik and the assistant director arrived at the movie set to see how things were progressing. "So, what do you think?" the assistant director asked Vik as they looked around the shabby set in dismay. It was supposed to resemble a grand palace. But it looked about as royal as a bus station.

"This is it?" Vik exclaimed. "This is my wedding set? Where are the flowers?" He leaned against a plastic column and the whole thing collapsed under his weight.

"Talk to your uncle," the assistant director told him. "He said this is all we could afford. We got that chair for free. Your uncle sure hates to pass up a bargain."

"Tell me about it," Vik complained, plunking himself down in the chair. That collapsed, too.

The cost-cutting had gone way too far, Vik decided. It was time to confront his uncle. Vik found him in his office and explained the situation.

"It's just not what I had in mind," he told his uncle. "None of it is."

Kamal sighed and sat back in his chair. "Vik, you need to learn some things about how the real world works," he told him.

"I went to film school, Uncle. NYU. I won awards. I know how to do this," Vik argued.

"Really?" Kamal said, raising an eyebrow. "You're over budget and behind schedule already. Do they give out awards for that?"

"Look, I just need some more time," Vik told him.

"Time is the one thing you don't have!" Kamal barked. "Another thing is money. So, if you don't start shooting next week, then I'm pulling the plug on *American Girl in India*."

"Actually," Vik said bitterly, "you titled it *Kamal Bhatia's Namaste Bombay*."

"I'm going to *re*-title it *Vik Bhatia's Bye-bye, Bombay, Hello, Dental School* if you don't fix this," Kamal growled.

"But the palace set is a wreck!" Vik exclaimed. "I can't have it ready in a week. What about a location?"

"If you think you can find one for free," said Kamal. "Otherwise, think about how many cavities you'll have to fill to pay off what we've spent so far."

*A* short time later, Vik walked into the studio commissary, where the Cheetahs and Amar were having lunch. The girls gave him

looks of pity. He looked really stressed out.

"No set," Aqua said, as he walked up to them. "I guess this weekend's auditions are off."

"I guess you heard," Vik said with a sigh. He ran his hands through his hair nervously. "I can't possibly find a location in a week, let alone for free. Uncle is going to shut down the movie for sure."

"Time to book our tickets home," Dorinda said.

"But you can't leave yet," Amar insisted, looking over at Aqua and taking her hand. "You haven't seen anything of India. Come home with me for Holi. It's my favorite holiday." He looked around the table. "In fact, you're all invited."

"What's Holi?" asked Chanel.

"It's the festival of colors," Amar explained.

"I can't go," said Vik, shaking his head. "I only have one week to audition, rehearse, and find a location."

"Trust me, Rajasthan is the perfect place to

find a location," Amar told him. "The village where my parents live is a hundred times more beautiful than any movie set." He paused and then added, "And I just might have a palace for you. You can rehearse, audition—I'll take care of everything."

Vik's eyes widened. "Wow! Thank you."

Amar patted him on the shoulder, then got up and headed out the door with Aqua.

"This is so exciting!" Chanel exclaimed. "Cheetah Road Trip!"

"Who is he?" Vik asked, pointing toward the door where Amar had just exited.

"Ah, he's with craft services," Dorinda fibbed. She didn't want Amar to get in trouble for hanging around the studio.

Just then, Kamal walked into the commissary. "Vik!" he yelled, spotting his nephew. "Why are you standing around? You have no set, and you only have a week left to prep."

"Uh, we were just making a plan to do some, uh, some location scouting," Vik told him.

"What do you know about location scouting?" Kamal exclaimed. "I'm coming with you."

The look on Vik's face made it clear that it was the last thing in the world he wanted. But Chanel and Dorinda were both grinning. They were about to have a whole new adventure!

*T*he next day, The Cheetah Girls woke bright and early to head out to Amar's village. As they loaded their bags into the cars that would take them there, Dorinda spotted the Swami sitting again beneath the wishing tree. She gave him a little wave.

"See ya later, Swami," she called.

"Don't forget to untie your strings," he replied.

"I think they'll stay there for a long time," Chanel told him. "Our wish doesn't look like it is going to come true."

"Ah, the tree is still working. You must give it time," said the Swami.

"Can you tell the tree to get a move on?" Dorinda joked.

"We're kind of running out of time," Chanel added.

"The point of time is to help you appreciate where you are," said the Swami, "not to make you rush to the next place. Understand?"

"Not really. No," admitted Chanel.

"Ah," said the Swami. "I have just the thing to make it more clear. One moment . . ." He reached for his banana leaf.

"Never mind. We get it. Thanks, Swami!" cried Dorinda, shoving Chanel along.

"Okay, let's get a move on," Aqua said. "We've got a long drive ahead of us."

As Chanel and Dorinda started for the car, Aqua lingered behind. When she knew the other girls weren't looking, she reached up and untied her string. Then she placed her hand on the trunk of the tree and mouthed the words, "thank you."

The Swami watched her curiously. Aqua smiled at him and put her finger to her lips. Then she tied the string into a bracelet and slipped it on to her wrist. She pulled her shirt-sleeve down to cover it and ran to catch up with her friends.

*A*mar's village was a few hours away, but to Chanel, the trip seemed to fly by. She stared out the window, unable to tear her gaze away from the view outside. They passed cows grazing peacefully in fields of tall grass, women in bright saris balancing baskets on their heads, and elephants bathing in a pond.

"This is amazing," Chanel said to Vik, who was sitting next to her. Aqua was sitting in the front seat with the driver, and Dorinda had hopped into another car with Rahim and Gita.

"Nothing like New York," Chanel added.

"I know. I grew up in Manhattan, too," Vik told her. "And most of my mom's family is there. They're from Colombia. I want to make this movie to show the other part of me, my father's family. This is the part of India—the countryside, the people, the colors . . ."

"So why don't you?" Chanel asked.

"Uncle wants to keep it safe. Make it commercial," Vik explained.

"Safe" sounded pretty boring to Chanel. She wondered why Vik even bothered with a movie that hardly seemed even to be his own. "What made you want to be a director anyway?" she asked him.

"When I was a kid, my parents used to take me to see movies all the time," Vik told her. "Sometimes we'd see Uncle's films, and it was the most amazing thing to think he made all of that happen. That he created those great stories. Now, when I write a script, I see the movie in my head. It's like I've met the characters and I've been to the places. I want the whole world to see my films."

"I get it," Chanel said knowingly. "It's like when I sing. It takes me somewhere else. I become someone else. It's the greatest feeling in the whole world, and I want to share it."

Vik looked into her eyes, and Chanel felt a little thrill.

I can't like Vik! she told herself, at least, not until the audition is over. She had promised her friends, and a promise was a promise.

But, oooh, he was so cute!

Meanwhile, in the other car, Kamal, sitting up front, was working on a budget. Dorinda sat between Rahim and Gita in the backseat. All three had books open, but no one was getting any reading done. Rahim and Gita kept stealing glances at each other, only to look away whenever they made eye contact.

Dorinda sighed. She lifted her book higher and tried to ignore them.

I hope we get to Amar's village soon, she

thought. If the tension in this car gets any thicker, it's going to explode!

*W*hen they reached the village, it was in the midst of a huge celebration. Everywhere they looked, people were singing and dancing and throwing colored powders into the air. It was a really amazing sight.

As they got out of the cars, Dorinda spotted an elephant standing nearby. It reached out its trunk and caressed Dorinda.

"My grandmother always says it's good luck when they kiss you," Gita told her. "They're trying to help you."

"Wait, like Ganesh?" Dorinda asked.

"Exactly! It's a sign. You're lucky," Gita explained. "They always ignore me."

Dorinda's face lit up. "Really? Maybe my luck *has* changed—" She broke off as the elephant showered her with a trunkful of water. "Or . . . not," she added, as her friends whooped with laughter.

As the group made their way through the village, colored powder rained down on them. Now the Cheetahs understood what Amar had meant by the "festival of colors." Chanel dipped her fingers in some orange powder and playfully threw it at Vik, who grinned.

Amar had said he would meet them at the dock, where a boat would take them to his house. When they arrived there, they found him standing with a whole group of people. Immediately, a dozen servants came up to the Mumbai group to carry their luggage away.

"So glad you made it!" Amar exclaimed.

Aqua's brown eyes widened at the sight of Amar. He was wearing a dazzling embroidered jacket and matching silk pants. He looked like a prince!

But before she could say anything, she was suddenly surrounded by Amar's mother and sisters. They danced around Aqua, singing and giving her sweets.

Wow, thought Aqua, loving the attention. If this is how they treat guests in India, I think I'll stay!

Amar took her hand, and as they walked together onto the boat, his sisters showered them with flower petals.

Chanel turned to Vik. "Did they just get married?" she asked.

"Oh, no," Vik replied with a laugh. "If this was a wedding, Amar would be riding a horse!"

It was late afternoon by the time the boat left the dock. The golden sunlight glimmered on the water and was reflected off a stunning white palace that sat on a hillside above the lake.

Aqua smiled as Amar took her hand. Suddenly she realized that the boat was sailing straight toward the palace. She turned to Amar in astonishment.

"Is that your palace?" she asked.

"Don't be ridiculous," Amar said, rolling his

eyes. He coughed, then added, "It's my parents'."

Aqua stared at him. I can't believe it, she thought. I've fallen in love with a prince!

12

*B*efore dinner, Amar took Aqua on a tour of the palace grounds. There were gardens with fountains, lush courtyards filled with flowers, and acres of land that included the lake they had sailed across to get there.

It was the most beautiful place Aqua had ever seen. But with each new surprise, she felt more annoyed.

"Why didn't you mention any of this?" she

asked Amar. "Were you just making fun of the smart girl who was too dumb to figure out you're a . . . what? A *Maharaja*?"

"I am no such thing," said Amar. "Technically. Until my grandfather dies." He sighed. "I probably should have mentioned that my dad owns the call center . . . *and* the phone company. And I think, maybe, the company that actually makes your phone. But he might have just sold that."

Aqua turned her phone over in her hand. "You should have told me," she insisted.

"I'm sorry," Amar told her. "But it doesn't change anything. I go to the school my father says I have to go to. I work at the call center because he insists I learn the business, whether I'm interested in it or not."

"That doesn't explain why you would leave all of this out," Aqua argued. "This is part of you."

"Yes, I know," Amar told her. "If anything, it makes my life more difficult. It limits my options."

"It looks like you have options," Aqua replied, eyeing a row of luxury cars parked in the driveway. "*Lots* of options."

"Not like you," said Amar. "If the Cheetahs don't work out, there are a million things you can do. You can make your own decisions. I can never do that."

"Have you even tried?" asked Aqua.

Amar shrugged. "That's just not how things work with my father."

"Amar!" his mother called through the window. "It's time to eat. Please let your friends know."

"Coming, *Ammaji*," Amar responded to her, calling his mother by the Indian name for mother. He took Aqua's hand and gave it a squeeze.

Aqua glanced up at the house, suddenly feeling nervous. "Is this, like, a big deal?" she asked.

"Don't worry," Amar told her. "It's just my family."

* * *

$\mathcal{J}$ust Amar's family turned out to be half the village—at least, that was how it seemed to Aqua! When the Cheetahs arrived in the palace dining room, they found at least twenty people around a huge table, all of them Amar's relatives.

"Welcome, everyone," Amar's mother said, smiling warmly. "We are so happy to be celebrating the holiday with you. Personally, I never imagined the day that Rahim Khan and Kamal Bhatia would be seated at our table!"

Rahim blushed. Kamal smiled smugly.

"And one other small thing," Amar's mother added. "I've prepared all of Amar's favorite dishes tonight. So, Aqua, pay close attention!"

Now it was Aqua's turn to blush as Amar's family laughed and clapped.

"Aqua, are you taking notes?" Dorinda teased.

Aqua smiled, embarrassed. "She's just being friendly," she whispered.

"I think she's being a little more than that," Chanel said.

Amar's mom leaned across Kamal and began to spoon some food onto Aqua's plate. "Aqua, how do you like the chicken tikka masala? I make it whenever Amar comes home."

Aqua smiled politely. "It's my favorite," she said.

"I'll give you the recipe later," Amar's mother told her.

"Don't worry," one of Amar's teenage cousins said to Aqua. "She did this to his last girl-friend, too." The girl winced as another cousin kicked her under the table. "Ow! She did!"

"I'm, um, not his girlfriend," Aqua told her.

"Not yet, at least," Dorinda quipped.

Aqua glanced down the table at Amar. He and Vik were deep in conversation.

I wonder what they're talking about, Aqua thought, watching them for a moment.

Probably just guy stuff, she told herself. And with a shrug, she dug in to her food.

"*T*his is incredible," Vik said to Amar. "It's just like the palace in *Namaste Bombay*! I mean, I wouldn't have asked if it weren't crucial, but do you think there's any chance . . ."

"That you could shoot here?" Amar asked. He grinned. "I don't think my mom would let Rahim leave if he tried! I'm sure she'd be thrilled."

"I hope so," Vik said. "Or else I'll be putting braces on twelve-year-old girls for the rest of my life."

"One thing," said Amar.

"For the guy who saved my movie? Anything. Name it," Vik said.

Amar smiled and leaned in to tell Vik what he wanted.

*T*he next day, Aqua was standing on the palace balcony, taking in the view, when Amar strolled up to her. "Guess who the newest member of the movie crew is?" he said.

"What? You're working on the movie now?" Aqua said in surprise. Between working at a call center and being a prince, doesn't he have enough to do already? she thought.

"Well, not really," he admitted. "But I *am* the location owner."

"Congratulations," Aqua said with a grin. Amar was such a sweetheart! He was totally helping Vik out.

"There was just one condition," Amar explained.

"What's that?" asked Aqua.

"That he cast you in the lead."

Aqua's smile faded. "But . . ."

"And don't worry about Uncle," Amar added. "I think I have a bit more pull now that I am the location owner."

Aqua didn't know what to say. She knew it was wrong for Amar to insist that she get the part. But it was hard to turn down the starring role in a movie.

Neither Aqua nor Amar realized that

Dorinda was standing on the balcony right next to theirs. And she'd heard every word.

Disgusted, Dorinda turned and stormed away. She strode along the palace terrace, not sure of where she was going. Moonlight shone on the marble floors, and a warm breeze ruffled her hair. There was no doubt that Amar's palace was beautiful. But Dorinda was too angry to appreciate it.

I can't believe Aqua! she fumed. So much for auditioning fair and square!

As she rounded a corner, Dorinda spied Rahim. He was dancing alone at the end of the terrace. "Hey, Mr. Superstar," she called out.

Rahim's head jerked up. He put a finger to his lips, signaling her to be quiet. He silently motioned to the courtyard below.

Dorinda followed his gaze. Gita was dancing in the courtyard, rehearsing the love duet from the movie. Now Dorinda understood: Rahim had been pretending to dance with Gita.

"Please tell me you're not doing what I think you're doing," Dorinda said, walking over to Rahim.

"I was just rehearsing," Rahim said casually.

"The other half of the love duet? By yourself?" Dorinda shook her head. "How long are you going to keep running away?"

"How long do I have?" Rahim joked.

"Do you really want to spend the rest of your life doing half the dance?" Dorinda asked him.

"What am I supposed to do?" Rahim replied. "I act like a total fool in front of her."

"It doesn't matter," Dorinda insisted. "None of that matters. If you really care about her, you've got to be willing to take that chance. You can't just keep hiding behind windows and archways and fake doors."

Rahim studied her for a moment. "You give pretty good advice," he said. "Ever take it yourself?"

Dorinda bit her lip. At the same moment,

her cell phone rang. Dorinda flipped it open. It was Joaquin.

"No," she told Rahim, flipping the phone shut.

Suddenly, her eyes filled with tears. Rahim put an arm around her. "Are you okay?" he asked gently.

Dorinda shook her head, unable to answer. As she did, laughter floated up from the rose garden below.

"Wait a second," Dorinda said, wiping her eyes. "What is *that*?"

Rahim shrugged. Together they looked over the side of the balcony. Chanel and Vik were strolling hand in hand past the rosebushes.

"See, I told you," they overheard Vik say.

"You're right. It *is* romantic," Chanel replied. Their voices rose up clearly to the balcony.

"They promised to play fair," Dorinda said angrily.

"Who? Chanel and Vik?" Rahim looked

surprised. "They're a couple, aren't they?"

"They *are*?" This was news to Dorinda!

"Well, everyone kind of thinks they are," Rahim told her.

"Has she been sneaking off with him this whole time?" Dorinda asked. "Why wouldn't she tell me?"

"Maybe she didn't want you to know. So that if she gets the part, you would think it was fair," Rahim said.

Dorinda couldn't believe Chanel would do that. But then again, the proof was right in front of her. She turned quickly and marched into the palace, with Rahim following.

Below in the garden, Chanel and Vik had no idea what had just taken place right above them.

"So, you think this would be a good place for the wedding scene?" Vik asked Chanel.

"Totally! This is incredibly romantic. But don't get any ideas," she added when she saw the look he was giving her. "We promised each other—no unfair advantages." She looked around at the beautiful gardens. "Is Amar going to let you shoot here?"

"Yeah, he said I could . . ." Vik told her, frowning.

Chanel smiled. She wondered why Vik didn't look happier.

Vik sighed. "But only if I cast Aqua in the lead," he explained.

Chanel's face fell.

"Don't worry," Vik said hurriedly. "I told him it wasn't up to me."

But it wasn't Vik that Chanel was worried about. "We all promised each other . . ." she began.

"Seems like you're the only one keeping that promise . . ." Vik told her. "The other Cheetahs aren't letting anything stand in their way." He checked his watch. "Well, I gotta turn in. I have to meet Rahim and Dorinda for dance rehearsal early tomorrow morning."

"Dorinda?" said Chanel. "Why is she rehearsing with Rahim?"

"He's helping her get ready for the audition," Vik told her.

"What?" Chanel's mind was churning.

"I keep telling you," said Vik, "you're the only one who's playing fair."

Chanel just stared at him. She couldn't believe what she was hearing. Her Cheetah sisters were totally cheating!

*T*he next morning, Dorinda and Rahim met in the courtyard to rehearse.

"So, what can I do to be more comfortable around Gita?" Rahim asked Dorinda as they danced together.

"You have to tell her how you feel," Dorinda told him. "Rehearsing with her would be a start."

Rahim shook his head. "I can't."

On the balcony above, Vik and Kamal watched them twirl around. "They look good together," Kamal said. "We should go with the dancer."

"But you've really got to listen to Chanel sing," Vik told him. "Uncle, I truly believe she's the one."

Neither Vik nor Kamal realized that Aqua was standing right behind them, listening to everything.

On the other side of the courtyard, Chanel was watching, too. When her eyes met Aqua's, both girls glared at one another. Each one thought the other was trying to get the part unfairly.

And now each was determined to get it for herself—at all costs!

*B*y the time of the audition later that day, the Cheetahs had barely spoken to one another since the previous night. As they gathered together on the upper balcony, ready to perform, tension filled the air.

Aqua bent down to tie her shoe when Chanel suddenly spotted the red string tied around her wrist.

"Wait a minute. What is *that*?" Chanel said, pointing.

Aqua glanced down at her wrist. "It's my string," she replied.

"From the wishing tree?" Dorinda asked.

"But our wish didn't come true yet," Chanel argued.

"Mine did," Aqua said defiantly.

"No, the movie isn't . . ." Suddenly it dawned on Chanel what Aqua was saying. "Wait. I wished for The Cheetah Girls to be the biggest movie stars of all time. What did you wish for?"

"I wished for The Cheetah Girls to stay together, exactly as we've always been," Dorinda said.

"Thanks for canceling out my wish, Do," Chanel snapped.

"Excuse me!" Dorinda shot back. "I was just trying to keep us from breaking up."

Chanel turned her head sharply. "That still leaves Aqua."

"Um," Aqua said nervously, "I wished that I would meet Kevin 347 in person."

Chanel's eyes narrowed. "Did you also wish

that your new boyfriend would buy you the part in the movie?" she snarled.

"What?" Aqua exclaimed. "I would never . . ."

"Spare us," Dorinda said, rolling her eyes.

Chanel turned around to glare at Dorinda. "Like you're so much better," she snapped. "I couldn't pry you away from Rahim with a crowbar."

What a hypocrite! Dorinda thought. "This, coming from the girl who wouldn't so much as bat an eyelash at the director!" she shot back.

"I didn't need to bat an eyelash," Chanel huffed.

Just then, Vik and Kamal walked into the room. Instantly the girls stopped squabbling.

Kamal sat down behind a table and folded his arms. "Are you ready?" he asked. "Who's first?"

Chanel stepped forward and began the song she had prepared. When she reached the end, she held a long note in the style of classical Indian music. Kamal looked impressed.

It was Dorinda's turn next. It hadn't taken her long to pick up some of Gita's Bollywood dance moves, and she worked them like they'd never been done before. Kamal nodded approvingly.

Finally it was Aqua's turn. She had prepared a monologue and she got so into it she cried at the end. Kamal smiled.

When the Cheetahs had finished, Kamal and Vik burst into applause. The girls sat down apart from each other. They nervously awaited Kamal's verdict.

Kamal stood up. "You're all great. I can see why you wanted to cast all three," he added, turning to Vik. "But we still can't afford it. So the role goes to . . ."

He paused. The girls held their breath.

"Chanel," Kamal announced, with a wink at Vik.

Chanel sprang out of her seat. She'd done it! She'd gotten the part! But her smile faded when she saw her friends' faces.

"Big surprise," Aqua snapped.

"Yeah, congratulations," Dorinda said sarcastically. "Fair and square, right?"

They stormed off, leaving Chanel feeling stunned and hurt.

Vik walked up to her with a smile. "Congratulations, Chanel," he said, handing her a script.

Chanel looked down at the script in her hands. Then, without a word, she turned and walked away.

*A*lone in the courtyard, Chanel paced back and forth, holding the script. Every now and again, she looked down and saw it in her hands. She knew she should have felt happy, but she didn't.

It isn't right for Aqua and Dorinda to be mad, she thought. After all, we auditioned, and I got the part. They had to pick *one* of us.

But had it really been fair? Chanel wasn't

sure. She didn't know how much Vik had influenced his uncle's decision. She would probably never know.

Just then, she looked up and saw Aqua and Dorinda come into the courtyard. And suddenly Chanel realized what she had to do.

"You were terrific, Chanel," Dorinda said sincerely. "I'm sorry about what I said. I didn't mean it."

"Me, too," said Aqua. "Chanel, you sang your heart out."

"Thanks, you guys," Chanel said gratefully. "But we were all great. And whatever happens, wherever we go, whatever we do, even though I know change is inevitable, we're still going to be Cheetahs. And Cheetahs never change their spots!"

Dorinda nodded and put her arms around her friends. "Cheetahs, say it like you mean it."

"Together," Aqua intoned.

"Now," added Chanel.

"And forever," the three girls said in unison.

"Ah, we're going to miss you," Dorinda said to Chanel.

"You're not gonna miss me that much," Chanel told her.

"What? Why not?" Dorinda and Aqua said at once.

"'Cause I'm not going to take the part," Chanel answered. "Nothing is worth losing you guys as my friends."

Aqua and Dorinda didn't know what to say. So they just wrapped her in a big hug.

*L*ater, Chanel found Vik and told him the bad news.

"So, you're all bowing out?" he asked her.

"Starring in a movie isn't worth destroying our friendship," Chanel explained.

Vik nodded, indicating that he understood. "Well, I'd better start writing," he said. "I have no idea how I am going to rewrite a love story without a love interest. But just give me a few hours." He sighed and added, "Uncle Kamal is going to freak out!" He picked up his script and began to scribble furiously.

Chanel put a hand on his arm. "I think it's time you stand up to your uncle," she said. "Make the movie you want to make. And if you can't, maybe this isn't the movie you should be making."

Vik put down his pen and looked at Chanel. "But what if this is my only chance?" he asked.

"It's not your chance if it's not the movie you want to make," Chanel replied. "Don't give up on your dream."

Vik pulled Chanel into his arms. "If you can't be my leading lady on-screen, maybe you'd consider playing the role in real life?"

Chanel smiled and put her arms around him. It was the only answer he needed.

"Too bad we're not at the Taj Mahal," Chanel commented.

"That can be arranged," Vik said, taking her hand as they walked off.

*M*eanwhile, on the terrace, Aqua and Amar were deep in conversation.

"Sorry for the mess," Amar told Aqua. "I was just trying to take your advice and make things happen."

"I meant for you to follow your dream. Not to try to buy mine." Aqua paused and then grinned. "But I think you're cute for trying."

Amar cocked an eyebrow. "One question. Would applying to Columbia count as following my dream? Because I talked to my parents, and they don't think it's the worst idea."

Aqua couldn't believe what she had just heard. Amar might go to her college? She screamed with excitement. She threw her arms around him and smiled.

"*Y*ou ready?" Dorinda asked Rahim.

"No," Rahim said nervously. "I'm scared. What if she doesn't like me back?"

Dorinda handed him a bouquet of flowers.

"Sometimes you've just gotta put yourself out there and not worry about what will happen."

Rahim took a deep breath. Holding the flowers behind his back, he walked toward Gita. But halfway there, he stopped. He looked back at Dorinda.

She gave him a thumbs-up.

Rahim nodded and walked up to the choreographer. "Gita?" he mumbled.

She turned, startled. As she did, she tripped over a huge brass vase.

"Oops, just ignore that," she said anxiously.

But the vase toppled into another, which crashed into another. Soon a whole row of vases had gone down like dominoes! The noise echoed throughout the whole palace.

Gita looked as though she might melt from embarrassment. But Rahim just laughed.

"You were saying?" Gita said, trying to act nonchalant.

Rahim pulled out the bouquet that he was hiding behind his back. "Do you want to have dinner with these flowers?" he began. He winced and tried again. "I mean, do your flowers want to have dinner with me?" He shook his head in frustration. "Aargh!"

"It's okay," Gita said, smiling. "I would love to have dinner with your flowers."

Rahim's eyes widened. "You would?"

Gita nodded. "Yeah, and I love the way you laugh," she said, taking the bouquet from his hands.

Dorinda watched them, grinning with satisfaction. All's well that ends well, she thought. Well, almost. She knew there was still one more thing she had to do.

Reaching into her pocket, Dorinda pulled out her cell phone and dialed Joaquin's number. He didn't answer, but she got his voice mail.

"Joaquin?" Dorinda said, taking a deep breath. "I'm sorry I've been avoiding your calls. We're in India; it's kind of a crazy story. Anyway, I've been doing a lot of thinking, and

I realize now that just because we're not going out doesn't mean we can't be friends. And I miss you. Call when you can. I promise I'll pick up."

Dorinda clicked off and sighed. She felt better than she had in weeks. She pulled out the statue of Ganesh that the Swami had given her and kissed its tiny trunk.

"Thank you for helping me realize I was the obstacle all along," she whispered.

"Look what I got for Vik," Chanel said to the Cheetahs later that afternoon. She held up a poster of a man and a woman embracing beneath a flower-covered archway. "It's an old movie poster of *Namaste Bombay*," she explained.

Aqua sighed. "I feel bad for him. Who's going to be the star of his movie?"

"Cheetahs?" Dorinda broke in. "Look."

The girls followed her gaze. Rahim and Gita were standing under an archway with their arms wrapped around each other. They looked just like the actor and actress in the movie poster.

The Cheetahs grinned at each other. They knew they were all thinking the exact same thing.

*S*oon after, Kamal was sitting by the pool sipping lemonade when the Cheetahs, Vik, Gita, Rahim, and Amar found him.

Kamal raised his eyebrows when he saw Vik. "You're still here?" he asked sarcastically. "Don't you have to go work on your application to dental school?" He had taken Chanel's decision to turn down the part as reason to cancel the movie altogether.

Vik ignored the comment. "We found the perfect lead for the movie," he told his uncle.

"So did I!" exclaimed Kamal. "Rahim in a wig. It's brilliant."

"No, Uncle Kamal," Vik replied. "It's Gita."

Kamal looked at Gita, who smiled shyly.

"That'll never work," he said gruffly. "No one wants to see the choreographer on-screen. That's why they are behind the scenes!"

Vik took a deep breath and looked his uncle in the eye. "She's a star," he said seriously. "And I'm going to prove it. This is my movie, and it's my one chance. So I have to do what I believe in . . ." He paused.

Kamal raised his eyebrows. "And?"

"And make a great movie," Vik finished confidently.

Kamal looked at his nephew as if he were seeing him for the first time. "Now you're sounding like a real director," he said proudly. "I've been waiting for this. Let's see what you got."

Vik grinned with relief.

The Cheetahs started cheering and jumped up and down.

"Come on, Gita!" Chanel said, putting an arm around her. "Let's get you Cheetah-fied!"

14

"*P*layback. And—action!" Vik shouted.

The cameras started to roll. As the music came up, the Cheetahs appeared! Vik had found a way to keep them in his movie as extras. They were dressed in fabulous Indian costumes and were flanked by dozens of dancers. After they finished an awesome singing and dancing routine, Gita and Rahim appeared. They were dressed as bride and groom, and they began a duet. Their voices were totally in sync.

As they finished their song, Rahim and Gita shared a kiss beneath a shower of rose petals. And even with the cameras rolling, Dorinda could tell from the look in their eyes that this kiss was real!

The Cheetahs and the other dancers continued to sing and dance and throw rice at the happy couple. And in the background were Amar and the Swami! Amar danced while the Swami hopped around and waved Dorinda and Chanel's red strings in the air.

Looking on, the whole film crew started to applaud wildly.

"Cut!" Vik yelled. "That was perfect!"

But no one heard him. Everyone was having such a good time they kept right on dancing and singing.

Well, Chanel thought as she looked around at all the smiling faces, it seems like this movie has a happy ending after all!